THE
THIRD
OPTION

CARSON BRANNAN

THE THIRD OPTION

ReadersMagnet, LLC

The Third Option
Copyright © 2022 by Carson Brannan.

Published in the United States of America.
ISBN Paperback: 978-1-956780-96-3
ISBN eBook: 978-1-956780-95-6

All rights reserved. No part of this publication may be reproduced, stored in a retrieval system or transmitted in any way by any means, electronic, mechanical, photocopy, recording or otherwise without the prior permission of the author except as provided by USA copyright law.

The opinions expressed by the author are not necessarily those of ReadersMagnet, LLC.

ReadersMagnet, LLC
10620 Treena Street, Suite 230 | San Diego, California, 92131 USA
1.619. 354. 2643 | www.readersmagnet.com

Book design copyright © 2022 by ReadersMagnet, LLC. All rights reserved.
Cover design by Ericka Obando
Interior design by Renalie Malinao

CONTENTS

Introduction vii

The Fair Winds 1
Lost and Found. 27
Mad-Man in Manhattan 37

Author's Post Script 49

INTRODUCTION

Like many, Jack Sloan was lost and drifting from job to job, until he found his passion. Call it fate, or serendipity. Some might even call it divine intervention. Whatever you call it, Jack stumbled across it, and his life changed forever. A lot of things would change in Jack's life, his marital status, where he would live, his occupation, and more. Jack Sloan, had learned a lot of things along life's highway, things that would help him on his journey down the road.

We don't always know where life is going to take us. It's sometimes like riding a rollercoaster blindfolded. There are a lot of ups and downs and some pretty significant turns. So, even though we may think we know where we are going to end up, sometimes fate has other ideas. This is where Jack found himself. Life had dealt him a hand that he didn't know how to play until Susan, a sailboat named Fair Winds, and Guy and Cheryl Atkins came into his life. From then on, it was an exciting ride, but one well worth taking.

THE FAIR WINDS

Mid-July 2009: somewhere in the southern Caribbean.
"Cheryl, get your life vest on and let's get topside. That storm in gaining on us and I don't want to get caught with our sails up."

"Right behind you, Guy."

"Quick, let's get these sails reefed in a bit in case the wind kicks up all of a sudden."

"Guy, look out!"

In the blink of an eye, a rogue wave almost capsized their boat and threw them into the sea; no food, no emergency beacon, only one bottle of water between them and a monster storm on the way.

Guy bobbed to the surface, not sure what had just happened.

"Cheryl! Cheryl where are you?" Just then he saw her flaming red hair come to the surface. Was she alright? Cheryl coughed and cleared her throat. Then she called out to Guy. Cheryl was all right, but the Fair Winds was sailing away and there was no way to catch her.

*****

It was a beautiful November day on St. Pete beach. The sun was high, and warm in the sky, the sea was a deep emerald green, and the air was a crisp sixty degrees. Jack and Susan Sloan were enjoying a walk on the beach. The sand was as fine, and white as sugar. As they stopped to gaze out over the Gulf of Mexico, Susan could just make out, on the edge of the horizon, the mast of a sailboat. The Sloans had only been married for three days and still had stars in their eyes, so one might not think it strange that she thought she saw something peculiar about the rigging on the sailboat. It appeared to the naked eye that there were several long streamers flying from the mast.

"Jack, is there a boat parade today?" Susan asked.

"Not that I know of, dear. Why?"

"There is a boat out there with a bunch of streamers flying from its mast," Susan replied.

"Where?" Jack queried.

"Right there," she said as she pointed towards the horizon.

Fortunately, Jack had brought along the top-of-the line binoculars they had received as a wedding gift. When he looked through the binoculars Jack could plainly see that those streamers were actually tattered sails. This struck him as strange since there had not been any storms or even strong winds in the area for at least a week. Susan noted, as she took a turn looking through the binoculars, that the boat appeared to be just drifting in the wind.

Jack had a thirty-two-foot Sea Ray named the Sea Stallion moored just across the island. Jack knew that Susan and he could get to the floundering sailboat even before the Coast Guard could get a chopper out to it, much less a surface vessel.

Five minutes later, the happy couple was racing, at flank speed, toward the stricken vessel. As Jack steered his craft out through the Pass-a-Grille channel, Susan was on the radio with the Coast Guard, giving them the details of the situation as best she knew them. It was determined that the Coast Guard would put a chopper on standby, but would not launch until Jack and Susan reached the sailboat and could determine if the chopper would be needed.

There was a six to eight knot wind out of the north west causing a slight chop on the gulf. Susan liked boating, but was not quite the seaman that Jack was. The pitching and yawing of the Sea Ray was starting to get to her and Jack knew it.

By now, their craft bad cleared the channel. Jack asked Susan to take the wheel and steer three hundred degrees true until she could see the sailboat. Then he wanted her to steer right for it.

Jack knew these waters well and he knew that there were no shoals this far from shore that could bother them. By keeping her mind occupied and constantly checking the horizon, Jack was hoping that Susan's queasy stomach would settle down. Not knowing what they might find on the vessel in distress, Jack didn't want Susan nauseous before they got there. Susan being a Registered Nurse, would, under normal circumstances, have a cast iron stomach, but the choppy seas had weakened her constitution.

The Sea Stallion, had been under way for about twenty minutes when Susan called Jack, in the cabin, to say they were fast approaching the disabled boat. After Jack turned over the helm to Susan, he had busied himself gathering up such things as the first aid kit, a flash light a flair gun, and just in case, he tucked a .32 under his shirt. He didn't want to alarm Susan, but being a former Navy SEAL Jack knew it was always better to be prepared for the unexpected than to have the unexpected take you by surprise.

Jack joined Susan on deck and they surveyed the sailboat. This was no little day-sailor; it was a forty-two foot Morgan. She was built for just about anything Mother Nature could throw at her. As they maneuvered closer to the boat, Jack asked Susan to throttle back and circle the stricken vessel slowly. There didn't appear to be any signs of life on board. Whatever had happened to this boat had been cruel and unrelenting. As the Sea Stallion crossed to the stern of the Morgan, Jack and Susan could clearly read the name. It was the Fair Winds. The couple immediately recognized the name. The Fair Winds had been missing and presumed lost in mid-July in the southern Caribbean. The story had been front page news for days following the disappearance of her and her high profile crew.

A sailboat lost at sea in the Southern Caribbean would not normally make the news in the States, but this was no ordinary boat. This boat belonged to Guy Atkins and his new bride, Cheryl. Guy Atkins and Associates had bid on and won the rights to drill for oil off of the coast of Florida. Guy had an uncanny knack for predicting when to abandon a venture and had ridden the IT and later the real estate bubbles with great success. He's said to be one of the wealthiest men in the world, not bad for a man who's barely forty. But now he and his bride were missing.

According to the news reports Guy had been born into money, in New York State. He went to all the finest schools and was groomed to be a gentleman. He joined the Air Force immediately after college. Guy climbed the ranks rapidly and was flying F18 Hornets by the time his father managed to persuade him to join with him in a philanthropic venture. Guy left the Service to work with his Dad, which launched him on a meteoric ride to wealth and fame.

Cheryl grew up in Connecticut, went to public school, and then a community college where she received a degree as a Registered Nurse. Susan had seen a television interview with the Atkins during which they discussed how they met. They met on a plane bound for the Poconos to do some skiing. Despite Guys notoriety, Cheryl had no idea who he was or that he was worth millions, if not billions. All she knew was that he was a gentleman and he had a cute smile. All Guy's money had not jaded him and he enjoyed being around a woman who liked him for himself and not for his money. One thing led to another, and eight months later, they were married.

Guy and Cheryl Atkins had set off on the Fair Winds for a three-month honeymoon cruise around the Caribbean. They departed from their home in East Hampton, New York, on June 15, 2009. They celebrated the Fourth of July at the Fountain Blue in South Beach, Miami, Florida. The next day, shortly after noon, they set sail for Puerto Rico, where they were to take on fuel, water, and supplies for the next leg of the trip to Jamaica. Jack Sloan remembered reading that the Fair Winds had arrived at the Puerto Prince Marina, Puerto Rico, on the evening of July 8. He had also read that the couple had been seen doing the tourist thing in Puerto Rico. They had gone night clubbing, taken a tour of the rainforest, and had managed to do some shopping in downtown Puerto Prince before getting about the business of restocking their boat. The last time anyone saw them, they were taking on supplies the evening of July 10. Their vessel was gone before daybreak on the morning of the eleventh.

On July 12, a low-pressure area just southeast of Puerto Rico developed into a hurricane and headed due west. When the Fair Winds did not arrive at the Kings Bay Resort and Marina, Jamaica as scheduled, the resort had tried to contact the Fair Winds by radio. After two days of no contact, the Jamaican Marine Authority was notified. When they found out who was on the Fair Winds, they contacted the U.S. Coast Guard. There was an immediate air and sea search by the U.S. Coast Guard, U.S. Navy, and the Jamaican Marine Authority. After a week of searching with no trace of the boat or its crew, the search was called off.

*****

The bad news is that on July 13, 2009 Guy and Cheryl were washed overboard and got caught up in the south side of the hurricane. The good news is, because they were south of the Hurricane, the winds and waves were pushing them ever closer to the Venezuela coast. By the morning of the third day the storm had passed them by and the coast of Venezuela was in sight.

"Guy I love you, but I don't think I can swim another stroke."

"Yes you can Cheryl. You didn't earn all those swimming trophies by giving up."

Even as the words were coming out of his mouth, Guy was thinking of the dozens of people around the world that drown in sight of land everyday.

Then he thought to himself, Not us! Not today!

*****

"Coast Guard Station Clearwater, this is the Sea Stallion, over."

"Go ahead, Sea Stallion."

"Coast Guard Station Clearwater, you are not going to believe this, but that sailboat we told you we were going to investigate is the forty-two foot Morgan, Fair Winds."

"Sea Stallion, please standby".

As they waited for the Coast Guard to radio back, Jack took note of the fact that both the main and the jib were up, so whatever happened, it had happened fast to the Atkins. The sails were shredded as though a giant beast had swiped its huge paw from bow to stern cutting the sails into ribbons. The hatches all seemed to be secured as though the couple knew something was coming, but they obviously didn't expect it to hit as quickly as it did. Jack thought to himself that the Atkins had most likely been washed overboard and would not have stood a chance in the type of weather that could do damage like this.

"Sea Stallion, Sea Stallion, this is Coast Guard Station Clearwater, over."

"Coast Guard Station Clearwater, this is Sea Stallion. Go ahead."

"Sea Stallion, could you standby the vessel until we can get Sea Tow out to your position, over?"

"Coast Guard Station Clearwater, this is Sea Stallion negative on your last. We can tow this vessel wherever you want it, over."

"Very well, Sea Stallion. Could you tow the Fair Winds to the John's Pass Marina? We will have personnel standing by for your arrival, over."

"Coast Guard Station Clearwater, this is the Sea Stallion affirmative on your last. It should take about three hours from this location, over."

"Three hours. Roger. Coast Guard Station Clearwater over and out."

After securing a line to the forecastle, the newlyweds were off. Jack had made the decision to let Susan steer most of the way, to which she had readily agreed, because the seas had not calmed down any and she felt better with her eyes on the horizon and the wind in her face.

The only trouble with steering a boat at sea is that it gives you a lot of time to think, and Susan was thinking about what might have happened to the Atkins. She had followed their story in the newspaper and felt she and Jack had a lot in common with the Atkins. They were about the same age, they all loved the sea, Guy and Jack had both been Captains in the military, and Cheryl was an RN just like Susan. Susan couldn't help feeling a kindred spirit with that couple who last strolled the decks of the ghost ship they had in tow.

Jack was sitting in the back of the boat, keeping an eye on the towline, and assuring that all was well. They had opted to steer straight for John's Pass instead of going back to Pass-a-Grille and taking the intercostal. The trip would be rougher but quite a bit shorter.

*****

Three days six hours and twenty minutes after being washed overboard, the Atkins crawled and clawed their way up on shore. Guy looked at Cheryl and took her hand. She mustered a smile then, exhausted, they both passed out.

Guy and Cheryl had survived being washed overboard and drifting for three days in the ocean. The rain and the clouds from the storm helped keep them from getting dehydrated, but their troubles were far from over. They had landed on a strip of coastline that was virtually uninhabited for a hundred miles in any direction.

*****

As the Sea Stallion and the Fair Winds entered the channel leading to John's Pass, Jack noticed the tide was flowing out of the pass. This meant they had to apply more power, but it also meant that the boat in tow would stay behind them as they navigated through the drawbridge. Jack had been through this bridge many times before in his Sea Ray, but they never had to open it for him. The Fair Winds was a different matter altogether. Her thirty-foot mast required the drawbridge to be fully opened before they dare attempt to ferry through it. Once through, they made their way to the John's Pass Marina.

Susan and Jack both spotted the men in uniform at the same time. Two Treasure Island Policemen and two Coast Guard Petty Officers along with one Coast Guard Captain were standing on the dock at Parade Rest, like five tin soldiers. Once docked, Jack and Susan joined the entourage who were now looking over the Fair Winds from the dock.

Captain Davis of the Coast Guard told Jack that under maritime law, the Fair Winds would become his property, once an investigation was completed to determine whether or not there had been a crime committed on the vessel. Jack's mind was spinning. He had not thought about salvage and the fact that he might end up owning this big beautiful boat with its teak decks and its mahogany interior. Where will we dock it? How much will it cost? Will we owe any taxes on it? His thoughts were interrupted by Susan throwing her arms around his neck, and planting a great big kiss on his lips. "Our very own sailboat," she squealed, but then sadly wondered what had happened to the previous owners. When Jack and Susan looked up, Captain Davis, the two petty officers, and the two policemen were aboard the boat being careful not to disturb anything but looking very intently all the same. Captain Davis and one of the policemen opened the main hatch leading from the cockpit to the main salon. They disappeared down the steps and were gone for what seemed like an eternity.

The policeman exited first and said, "All appears shipshape down below, but we'll let the folks from the crime lab have a look just to be sure."

By now, there was a large crowd of onlookers gathering on the dock. The two policemen quickly produced a roll of yellow tape, which had written on it in big bold letters, "Crime Scene Keep Out." They proceeded to wrap the tape from stem to stern on the Fair Winds and then they took up guard positions in front of the gangplank.

Captain Davis took down contact information from Jack and Susan and told them, "As soon as I know anything I'll let you know." With that, Jack and Susan boarded the Sea Stallion and took the inland waterway back to Pass-a-Grille.

Surprise, surprise, the press found out about the Fair Winds and they were on it like bees on honey. By the time Jack and Susan turned on the evening news, all the local channels, and most of the cable news net works already had crews on sight at John's Pass Marina, satellite trucks and all.

"Susan, pack a bag and let's get out of here." "Why, Jack? We just got home."

"Because, Sweetheart, it won't take long for the press to find out, who the Sea Stallion is registered to, and that will bring them right to our door." Without another word spoken by either of them, they were packed and gone within fifteen minutes.

Susan registered them into a pay by the week motel under her maiden name to throw the press off the scent. It wasn't home, but it was better than having to put up with the press twenty-four-seven. Within two weeks the hoopla died down and the press lost interest in the Fair Winds, making it safe for Jack and Susan to move back home.

Captain Davis had, as promised, kept Jack and Susan abreast of what was happening with the investigation. On January 10, 2010, it was determined by a maritime judicial review board that there was no evidence of foul play on the Fair Winds, clearing the way for Jack to take possession of her under maritime salvage laws. Guy and Cheryl Atkins were both only children and their parents were no longer living; therefore, since the Atkins had been lost at sea and presumed dead there was no one to challenged Jack and Susan's right to take possession of the Fair Winds. On February 10th, one month to the day after the board gave its ruling, and having received no challenges to the ruling, the board released the Fair Winds back to the Coast Guard. Captain Davis immediately called Jack to let him know that he now owned the Fair Winds, and that he had two days to move the vessel from the docks at John's Pass Marina or he would be charged docking fees.

Susan was at work when Jack got the call. He decided to surprise Susan, so he called her up and told her that he wanted to pick her up and go to dinner after her shift.

When he picked her up, he drove her to Madeira Beach, and then turned left. They proceeded south over the John's Pass Bridge.

Susan was curious just where Jack was taking her for dinner, so she asked, "Are we going to the Hurricane?" Jack said nothing.

"How about the Wind-Jammer?" Still, Jack was silent. The vehicle turned left just past the bridge and then Susan was sure she knew.

"We're going to Gators, aren't we?" Jack drove straight by Gators.

This confused Susan, and she said, "Hey fella, I thought you were taking me to dinner."

"I am; just thought you might like to have dinner on your new boat." Susan had been so involved in the conversation that she had not noticed that Jack had turned into the parking lot at John's Pass Marina.

When she looked up, right in front of her was the Fair Winds. It had flags flying fore and aft.

All Susan could say was, "Wow!" and then she started crying like a little girl.

Jack hated to see Susan cry, but on this occasion, all he could do was laugh because he knew these were tears of joy, not pain. Dinner was not all that happened on the Fair Winds that night.

The interior of the boat was luxurious yet functional. The woodwork was all mahogany and the seat cushions were covered with high-end stain resistant microfiber. The galley had a gas stove and oven. There was a microwave and a refrigerator which was larger than the norm for a boat this size. The V-berth in the bow of the boat was nice but the Captain's cabin in the aft part of the boat reminded Susan of a sultan's palace. The sheets were satin and the curtains covering the portholes were imported silk. "Jack, I love this boat. She is the most beautiful boat I've ever seen and to think she is ours is almost beyond belief, but I wish those two people didn't have to die so we could have her."

"I know Sweetheart that really sucks, but death is part of life and all any of us can do is to be prepared to meet our maker when our time comes." Susan nodded in agreement then laid her head on Jack's shoulder and gave a faint sigh.

*****

Guy's survival training was paying off in spades. Cheryl and he had not been hungry once since they landed on the northern coast of Venezuela. The northern coast of Venezuela is only ten degrees off of the equator and the animal and plant life .is abundant. The down side is that it is always hot and humid with plenty of poisonous plants, snakes, and insects to content with. Thank God, Guy always kept a knife tied to his belt. It had proven invaluable on numerous occasions. Like the time Cheryl twisted her ankle and Guy had to fashion a splint and a crutch out of a sapling in the jungle. Or the time he made a spear so they could have Iguana for dinner.

*****

One more day to move the boat, with dock space at a premium in the bay area and the prices high accordingly. Jack and Susan weren't sure what they were going to do. Jack had been making ends meet by cleaning boat bottoms and since Susan moved in, the cash flow had greatly improved, but time was as short as dock space, so Jack and Susan decided to anchor Fair Winds in a small bay behind the VA Hospital. There were between eight and ten boats anchored in the bay at any one time. Fair Winds was the largest boat in the bay and she looked like a mother hen with her brood gathered around. The bay was a little shallow for a boat of her size and at very low tide her keel would rest on the soft bottom and she would keel over just slightly.

Jack and Susan did a thorough inventory of Fair Winds and found to their delight that Guy and Cheryl had outfitted her very well indeed. The boat had two of everything, including sails. The sails that had been tattered in the storm had been fair weather sails. They found her storm sails still neatly stowed in the sail locker.

As they were looking around the captain's cabin aft of the main salon, they came across Guy and Cheryl's personal affects. Jack and Susan couldn't help but wonder what exactly happened to them. Among the items in the cabin Susan found Guys Air Force ring and a wallet size copy of Cheryl's nursing license. She also found a bottle of very expensive French perfume. She felt strange, almost as if she was doing something wrong, when she slowly slid the stopper out of the bottle releasing the most alluring fragrance she had ever smelled. In an instance the whole cabin was filled with the most heavenly fragrance and she quickly resealed the bottle.

As Jack continued looking around the interior of the boat he found the ship's logbook tucked in the back of a drawer at the navigation station. As Jack read it, he could tell, by the entries, that Guy was not only an accomplished sailor but also very detail oriented. The last entry in the log was 0800 the morning of July 13, 2009. It gave their exact longitude and latitude and Guy had stated that they knew the storm was coming and they had decided to steer south by southwest to try and avoid it.

Jack pondered that last entry, he wondered if they could have made it to a cove somewhere and the boat had broken free from its moorings leaving them stranded, but that wouldn't explain the ripped sails. Then he wondered if they had failed in their effort to out run the storm and been washed overboard and drifted on the currents possibly to an island or the Coast of Venezuela. The more he thought about it the stronger the feeling became that the Atkins just might be alive. He shared his thoughts with Susan and almost without thinking she was on board with his theory.

*****

While Guy and Cheryl were crossing a small stream, Guy was bitten on the leg by a poisonous water moccasin. He quickly cut the area with his knife and squeezed as much of the venom out as he could. Cheryl set up camp close to the stream and spent the next week nursing Guy back to health. The first twenty-four hours were pretty scary. Fortunately, Guy had managed to squeeze out most of the venom and Cheryl had learned a lot about living off of the land by the time Guy crossed paths with the snake. While Guy was out of commission she built a shelter out of banana leaves and saplings, built a fire, and gathered food from the jungle. She speared a fish and even put a poultice of herbs and mud wrapped in banana leaves over Guy's snake bite to try and draw out the poison. By the third day Guy was able to help her by giving her information on other plants to use for food and medicine. It was a close call, but Guy was just fine after about a week. The down side is that it cost them a week of travel towards civilization.

*****

Susan and Jack spent every spare moment, when they were not working, going over the weather reports, tide and current charts for the area southeast, south, and southwest of Jamaica during the period of July 13 through 17, 2009. Jack figured without provisions or a lifeboat, three or four days would be as long as Guy and Cheryl could have survived at sea. Jack knew that there was a great deal of the Venezuelan coastline that was uninhabited, and if they had washed up along there, they could still be alive. The climate was mild and food was abundant, if you knew where to look. Jack knew that as a Captain in the Air Force, Guy would have had survival training. So the chances would be very good that, if they had made it to shore, they could have survived.

When Jack and Susan were awarded ownership of the boat they decided they had two options; they could sell the Fair Winds, which would have made them a pretty penny, or they could keep the Fair Winds and just go on with their lives, but after reading the ship's log Jack and Susan realized there was a third option, which was to sail the Fair Winds down to the southern Caribbean in an attempt to locate Guy and Cheryl Atkins. The third option soon became the only option the couple would contemplate.

> Ships log March 01, 2010: 0800, Key West, Florida. We have just topped off our fresh water and food supplies and are about to get underway for the southern Caribbean.

Jack had told Captain Davis of their plans, despite the Captain's objections to the plan, based on the fact that the Coast Guard, Navy and The Jamaican Marine Authority has spent a week and found nothing, and the fact that no one has seen any evidence of the Atkins since their disappearance. Not to mention that it was going to cost Jack and Susan a good deal of money to go on this wild goose chase. He was good enough to clear the expedition with the Venezuelan consulate. With Their visas and passports in order Susan had taken a month off of work and her boss told her she could have more time if she needed it. Jack let his customers know he would be unavailable till further notice.

> Ships log March 06, 2010: 1600, Kingston, Jamaica. After giving Cuba a wide berth so as not to have any trouble with the Cuban authorities, we have arrived in port to take on supplies before setting off on the searching leg of this voyage.

After a hot shower in the dockside locker rooms, Jack and Susan set out to take in the local culture and some of the famous Jamaica cuisine. Up till that point, the Fair Winds had been enjoying just that, fair winds. The voyage thus far had been uneventful, save the occasional, school of dolphin playing around the bow of the boat and those phenomenal star-filled nights when the Milky Way looked like God had taken a paint brush and passed it over a black velvet canvas leaving millions of sparkling diamonds in its wake. Sunrise and sunsets in the open sea are something one cannot adequately describe in words, with all their hues of pink and red and orange and yellow against a back drop of every thing from bright iridescent blue to shades of purple and black, but once witnessed, can never be forgotten. Well, all of that was about to change.

Two days out of port from Jamaica the weather took a definite change for the worse. Jack thought to him self, how strange it is that the sea can be calm and the weather clear one hour and an hour later she is angry and the sky is dark. Susan, was not doing well with her sea-sickness, but she was a real trooper and never missed a beat while reefing in the sails and battening down the hatches. Jack turned the Fair Winds into the wind and put out a sea anchor because the wind was too strong and the seas were too big to try and sail her, the best Jack could do was keep her bow pointed into the wind. She'd ride over one wave and try and dive under the next. This would cause her to shutter and Jack and Susan would get a face full of sea spray. The Fair winds was built for just such a scenario and Jack knew she had been through worse storms than this and survived so he had every faith that she would survive this one. Jack and Susan wore their life jackets and tied safety lines to themselves. Susan elected to stay topside with Jack during the storm partially because of her seasickness and partly because she didn't want to be trapped below if the Fair winds started sinking. The wind and waves pushed them ten miles backwards before the storm passed. Three hours after it started it was all over and the sky had turned back to blue without a trace of the storm they had just endured. It took another hour for the sea to calm down, but Jack and Susan both knew without saying it that they owed their lives to how well the Fair Winds was built.

> Ships log, March 20, 2010: 1800, two hundred yards off the coast of Venezuela. Ten days of searching and still no sign of Guy and Cheryl Atkins. Susan and I have spoken to several fishermen but none have seen the couple. Maybe we'll have more luck tomorrow. Thanks to time and copious amounts of ginger, Susan seems to have overcome her problem with seasickness. She has no trouble going below and whipping up a quick meal while underway and enjoys the gentle rocking of the boat at anchor as she reads a book or snuggles into bed for the night.

On the twelfth day, Susan spotted a large fishing trawler on the horizon. It was a deep-sea trawler that could not come in as close as Fair Winds to shore.

Jack radioed the trawler," Deep Sea Fishing Trawler this is the sailing vessel Fair Winds. Do you read, over?"

"This is the trawler Grenada Princes. We read you loud and clear, over."

"Grenada Princes have you seen anything unusual along the shore over the last few months, weeks, or days, over?"

"Fair Winds this is the Captain of the Grenada Princes and I have personally seen a single campfire on the shore far from any villages on many occasions. Every time I see it, it seems to be farther to the west than it was the night before. I assumed it was a fishing party camping for the night, over."

"Grenada Princes could you give me the location where you last saw the fire and when that may have been, over?"

"Fair Winds the location would be approximately twenty nautical miles west of your current location. The last time I saw the fire was about a week ago, over."

"Grenada Princes I really appreciate your help. Good luck with your fishing. Fair Winds over and out."

"Good luck to you also Fair Winds. Grenada Princes over and out." As it turned out, the location the Captain had given them was one that Jack and Susan had not searched yet. This gave them hope. The beach was a three-hour sail from where they were, but the anticipation made it seem like twice that long. Finally, the Fair Winds arrived. Jack maneuvered the boat as close as he dared to shore and then they dropped anchor.

After making sure the anchor was holding, Jack and Susan went about lowering the Zodiac inflatable dingy over the side and mounting the outboard on the back. With their hopes high, Jack and Susan headed for shore. After about twenty minutes of combing the beach, Susan heard Jack excitedly calling. She ran to him as fast as she could. Jack was standing over a bed of coals in the sand. The coals appeared to be several days old and the wind and tide had swept away any foot prints that might have been there. Jack and Susan had seen other campsites where fishermen had stopped for the night, but unlike the others, there was no telltale trash around the area at this campsite. They couldn't be sure, but they had a good feeling about their find.

"Guy Atkins! Cheryl!" Two hours of yelling and searching. Jack and Susan's throats were raw and they were out of water.

"Let's call it a day, Susan. We'll stay at anchor here for the night and see if anyone returns to the beach."

"Okay, that sounds like a plan. Besides, I can't yell anymore," Susan said.

The Caribbean offered them another amazing sunset, but by ten o'clock the rain was blowing sideways. Susan was eating ginger tablets like they were going out of style in an effort to calm her stomach. Even if someone wanted to have a fire on the beach that night, it would have been impossible.

The storm had blown itself out around midnight and an eerie calm had settled over the small bay where Fair Winds was at anchor. With the humidity off the scale and not a breath of air, sleep was out of the question. So, when dawn broke, Jack and Susan were top side, weary, but wide-awake. The coast of Venezuela in this area was rough and unforgiving. It was a mixture of sand and sharp slippery rocks.

Jack thought that if Guy and Cheryl had been here, they might be on the move. Because the coast was so hard to traverse and the sun was so unrelenting at this latitude, they might move inland during the day and come back to the beach at night for some relief from the heat, and for the chance to be spotted by passing fishermen. Jack also surmised that Guy would know that if he kept going west he would find civilization. Jack discussed his thoughts with Susan and the decision was made to weigh anchor and head west along the coast.

Was the campfire two days old or a week? Could Guy and Cheryl travel two miles a day or ten? Was that camp fire even theirs? These were all question that were racing around in Jack's head. Susan seemed content to follow Jack's lead. He had been doing a pretty good job so far. Jack elected to travel about five miles down the beach and anchor out about a thousand yards. He deduced that at that range, they could survey roughly ten miles of the shoreline at a time. Of course, this did not take into account numerous rock outcroppings that could easily hide a campfire. The plan wasn't perfect but it would have to do. Neither their time nor their money was endless. Jack couldn't help but think, if the shoe was on the other foot and it was Guy and Cheryl looking for Susan and me, money would be no object. But then again, why would Guy and Cheryl ever find themselves looking for us?

After fourteen days there was still no sign of Guy and Cheryl.

"Two more days and we are going to have to break off the search and resupply."

"I know Jack. We are just about down to peanut butter and crackers. Call it woman's intuition, but I feel good about tonight. I think we're going to spot something."

"I sure hope your right, sweetheart."

"I'm about over this three-hour cruise."

"Good one Jack."

"Seriously, Susan, I'm beginning to think that Captain Davis was right.

"Jack, Let's give it two more days then we'll look at where we're at. Ok?

Jack shrugged his shoulders in response and went back to what he was doing.

The sun was about to dip into the crystal blue sea, the winds were light, the anchor was holding, Jack and Susan had just finished dinner, and were getting ready to start watching the beach for camp fires when;

"Look Jack! On the beach!"

"Where?"

"Over there, about twenty degrees off the starboard bow!"

Jack grabbed his binoculars, the same ones he had used the day Susan and he had found the Fair Winds. There on the beach were two people, a man and a woman, waving for all they were worth. Jack thought to himself, could it be? Could we have just found the long lost billionaire and his bride. Not so fast, he thought. We are quite a ways off shore. That could be just a young couple having a good time and waving hello. No, these people were frantic. They had already waded out into the surf, up to their chests and it looked like they were trying to decide whether they could swim all the way out to the boat. Jack quickly exchanged the binoculars for a bullhorn.

"Stay where you are. We will come to you. Go back on shore and wait."

Susan was already unlashing the Zodiac. Jack and Susan had it in the water and ready to go in record time.

Susan couldn't help herself. She just had to say it, "I told you I had a feeling about today."

"Well, if this turns out to be who we think it is, I'll never doubt your woman's intuition again," said Jack.

Really tan and sporting a nine-month-old beard it was him. The one and only Guy Atkins, billionaire: entrepreneur, soon-to-be oil tycoon and his very tan, rather thin, slightly disheveled bride, Cheryl.

"By all the stars in the heavens, how did you find us?" asked Guy.

"By the grace of God and woman's intuition I'd say," replied Jack.

The sky had gotten cloudy and the wind was picking up. It's not unusual to have an afternoon shower almost every day at this latitude. So the group wasted no time boarding the Zodiac and heading back to the boat.

"That boat looks just like our boat, the Fair Winds," Guy said.

"That's because it is, the Fair Winds." said Jack. "Let's get you two on board, cleaned up, and give you some food. Then we can fill you in on what has happened since you decided to take a little swim in the ocean." This brought a hearty round of laughter from everyone on the dingy.

After a fresh water shower, shave, and a hearty meal, Guy and Cheryl, told the Sloans how a rogue wave had nearly capsized the Fair Winds and had swept both of them overboard. Thankfully, they had donned life jackets before going topside, because they knew the outer bands of the hurricane would be hitting them soon. The wave caught them totally off guard, since the sun was bright and the sky was still a rich Caribbean blue. They spoke of how they had survived at sea for three days before being washed up on the north coast of Venezuela and their subsequent ordeal in the jungle until spotting the Fair Winds.

Guy said, "If it hadn't been for the fact that Cheryl tied a bottle of drinking water to her life-preserver before we went top side, we would have never made it to shore alive."

Cheryl piped in, "Well, if Guy wasn't such a Tarzan when it comes to surviving in the jungle, we would have starved to death within a week."

Guy, blushed and then continued, saying, "The forest was teaming with small birds and animals that had little fear of humans. There was plenty of fruit and other vegetation that was not only edible, but delicious. On one occasion I was able to kill a four-foot iguana with a spear I fashioned out of a piece of bamboo."

Cheryl interrupted and said, "It tasted like chicken and we ate off of it for two days."

Guy said, "The biggest threat to our lives would have been a chance encounter with a jungle cat or a poisonous snake or insect. Thankfully we never crossed paths with a cat and we were able to avoid all, but one poisonous snake." He lamented, "We would try, when ever possible, to camp on the shore at night where we would build a big signal fire, and time and again we would see boats passing in the night, but none would ever stop."

Jack and Susan told of how the Fair Winds had drifted on the currents in the Gulf of Mexico until they saw it just off shore of St. Pete Beach and the circumstances that had brought them to be a thousand feet off the coast of Venezuela on that fateful evening.

The next day they would set sail for Jamaica. Jack and Susan had graciously given up the captain's cabin to Guy and Cheryl the first night on board. For which Guy thanked them profusely. Jack and Susan appreciated having two more people to help crew on the Fair Winds. She was a well-appointed vessel, but many hands make light work. Guy was on deck along with Jack, at first light, weighing the anchor and setting the sails. The wind was blowing at about ten knots out of the west-northwest, which made for some fine sailing and no need to tack in order to make way for Jamaica. The ladies, in the meantime, busied themselves in the galley making breakfast for the crew. All that the four of them did, or didn't, have in common, made no difference at all. They all became close friends seemingly overnight. Within days, they were telling each other their deepest secrets. The four of them shared a good sense of humor and the rigging on the boat would resonate to the sound of laughter that emanated from the cabin night after night. It was not all fun and laughter though. Once they were within radio range of Jamaica, Jack radioed the news of the miraculous discovery of Guy and Cheryl Atkins. By the time the Fair Winds was within sight of the coast of Jamaica, there was a whole armada of boats, of all sizes, filled to the gunnels with reporters and photographers all trying to be the first to get the story of the rescue of the Atkins. This consequently, plunged Jack and Susan Sloan into the limelight. Jack was not comfortable being the center of attention and Susan felt about the same.

Within twenty-four hours of their arrival in Kingston, Jamaica, some of the top executives from Guy's company arrived to talk to him and take charge of the PR work. After a week of nonstop press conferences and television interviews the press crews started to lighten up. There were still photographers and the occasional autograph seeker, but all in all, it was much more pleasant to walk down the streets of Kingston than it had been since their arrival.

Jack and Susan discovered upon arriving in Jamaica that their money was no good. Anything they wanted to buy was either given to them by the merchant or was taken care of by Guy and Cheryl. It's not everyday that someone saves the life of arguably one of the wealthiest men in the world and his lovely bride.

Guy and Cheryl flew back to New York from Jamaica and Jack and Susan sailed back to St Petersburg, Florida. This was the end of one chapter in the lives of these four wayfarers, but by no means the end of their story.

*****

Five years and two thousand nautical miles from where they first met, Guy, Cheryl, Jack, and Susan's lives had changed forever. Guy proved to be as generous as he is wealthy. Guy and Cheryl were so happy and grateful to Jack and Susan for taking the time out of their lives to search for them, when everyone else had written them off for dead; not only did they not ask for the Fair Winds back, but when they found out that Jack wanted to be a reporter, Guy fixed him up with a Job at The New York Sentinel, where Guy owned 51 percent of the stock. This meant that Jack and Susan would have to move; so Guy built them a home close to Cheryl and him in East Hampton and gave it to them free and clear. Cheryl, being as independent as she is beautiful, had opted to keep working even after marrying one of the wealthiest men in the world. It didn't take much talking to get Susan a job at the same hospital that Cheryl worked for. The two couples had become best of friends and spent many pleasure filled weekends on the Fair Winds. Susan and Jack often wonder how different their lives would have been had they not taken the third option, and they wondered where would life lead them from here.

LOST AND FOUND

Guy Atkins was able to get Jack Sloan a job as a reporter with The New York Sentinel, but it was up to Jack to keep it. Jack had been lost and adrift on the sea of life, never finding a job that seemed to fit, since his untimely medical retirement from the military. He was intelligent and very talented. Jack could fix or build just about anything, but he had always wanted to be a reporter. Not a journalist per se, but an investigative reporter, and solving the case of the missing billionaire couple just added fuel to that fire. Well, here he was, working his dream job, but not exactly. As with any new reporter, and particularly one with no prior experience in the field, he was assigned to new school openings, park dedications, charity functions, and the like. This was not what he had signed on for, but he was smart enough to realize that you have to crawl before you walk, and you have to walk before you run. So Jack Sloan, reporter par-excellence, was resigned to his position as a human interest reporter, for now.

Jack had been doing his job for eight months, two days, and four hours (not that anyone was counting) when he got his first big break. He had been gathering information on the restoration of a historical neighborhood in the Bronx. He had just mounted the front steps of a Victorian style house with gray slate siding and white gingerbread trim. It had some well manicured bushes that partially hid the porch from the street. On the left side of the porch was a beautiful fountain containing goldfish. He was just starting to snap some pictures when the walkie-talkie size police scanner that he wore on his hip, started blurting out details about a bank robbery that had just happened a few blocks from his location.

"Two male subjects, both white, one over six foot, the other five eight to five ten. Subjects driving an older model, blue Cadillac last seen heading south on Vine towards the Bentwood neighborhood," The female police dispatcher said in a thick New Jersey accent.

All right, he thought, this scanner I bought is going to help me get into the big leagues. Jack was tempted to drop what he was doing and take a run over to the bank. He knew he would be the first reporter on the scene, because the bank was only about a mile away. He thought better of the idea, and went back to what he was doing. He had barely turned back around when a dark blue, older model Cadillac came flying into the neighborhood, tires squealing. The car pulled up right across the street from where Jack was doing his report. Where Jack was standing on the porch, the view of the occupants of the vehicle was obscured by a large bush. Jack, on the other hand, had a clear view of them and soon realized that the two guys in the car were probably the bank robbers. The ski masks they were wearing, in the middle of June, pretty much gave it away. Jack quickly turned down the volume on his police scanner and started snapping pictures with his company issued Nikon digital camera. The police were apparently unaware of the robbers' location because five minutes later, there was still no sign of them. The robbers, however, had been very busy. They had tried to gain entrance to the house directly across the street from Jack. It was vacant, but very well sealed.

The house was built in a horseshoe shape with a courtyard in the middle, facing the front. In the courtyard was a large, ornate fountain that had long since run dry. The robbers were two white men in their thirties. One was tall, about six foot four with a shaved head, and the other was about five foot eight with sandy blonde hair. The camera the paper had issued to Jack was very good indeed. From his vantage point behind the bush, he was able to snap some gallery quality pictures of both of the robbers' faces and of the tattoos they were both sporting. The robbers disassembled the fountain, which was hollow inside. There, they stashed the loot from the robbery along with the masks they had used.

Jack used his cell-phone to call the police. He suggested they roll in under silent alarm mode and gave them the address. The robbers thought they had pulled off the perfect crime until they emerged from the courtyard only to be staring down the barrels of six pistols and two shotguns.

The headline of The New York Sentinel the next day read, Bank Robbers Arrested After Anonymous Tip.

"Jack, your first headline," Susan yelled as she ran up the driveway with the paper in one hand and spilling most of the content of her morning coffee out of the cup in her other!

"I'm so proud of you I could just bust."

The story and photos had not escaped the editor's attention, but it takes more than one lucky catch to make a true reporter.

Two months later, Jack got a call from the Editor and Chief of the paper.

"Jack I'm going to give you a shot at a big story. There is a dam on the Passaic River, near Garfield. It has been weakened by the recent rain and it looks like it may fail. Do you think you can handle that?"

"Hell yeah! Thanks, Boss. You won't be disappointed," Jack exclaimed.

Jack could hardly wait to get to his car so he could call Susan. When the phone at the hospital was answered, Jack asked, "May I speak to Susan Sloan please? She is on the IC unit."

"Who shall I say is calling?" The voice on the phone came back.

"Jack Sloan," he replied.

"Hi, Dear," Susan said with a smile in her voice. "I was just thinking about you. What do you want for supper?"

Jack replied, "I may not be home for supper. That's what I'm calling you about. I just got a big assignment from the editor of the paper to cover a possible dam breach near Garfield."

With obvious excitement in her voice Susan said "Honey that's great news, but do be careful. Promise?"

Jack responded almost without thinking, "Of course I will."

Susan's voice, more insistent, "Promise!"

Jack, now realizing the extent of Susan's concern, replied much more solemnly, "I promise. I've got to go. Love You."

"Me too," Susan replied. Then she heard the phone go silent.

The dam in question had been built in the 1940s. It had stood strong, through ice and wind and rain for some seventy years, but it was getting old and it didn't take an expert to see it was showing its age. There had been a plan on the books to build another dam just downstream from this one during the dry period the next year. From the looks of things, this dam wouldn't last that long. Fortunately, there weren't too many settlements directly on the river. The river had a bad reputation for being flood prone, and most of the banks and mortgage brokers won't lend construction money for any homes or businesses to be built on the flood plain of the Passaic.

When Jack arrived, he could see that the floodgates were wide open but the water was still going over the top of the dam. The sound was deafening. It reminded Jack of the sound people describe when a tornado is coming. He saw three choices when he got there. He could have parked at the base of the dam and taken some amazing photos of the water cascading over the top, or he could have stood on the catwalk at the top of the dam and taken some equally amazing photos, or he had a third option; he could do as he promised and stay out of harm's way. Jack was a man of his word and he would die before he would break a promise to his wife. So, Jack found a place to park, high on a ridge over looking the dam. It allowed him a bird's eye view of the dam and the valley below. With the telephoto lens on his camera, he was able to take even more dramatic pictures than he would have been able to get from the other two spots, and still remain safe.

Jack learned, from some of the people that had gathered on the ridge with him, that years ago the authorities had installed a dam break early warning system in the valley. It consisted of a series of horns that would blare once every fifteen minutes if the dam appeared to be in danger of failing, once every minute if a breach appeared immanent, and continuously if the dam failed. By the time Jack arrived, the horns were sounding every minute. Despite the fact that most of the financial institutions would not loan money for construction on the flood plain of the Passaic, there were a few hardy souls that couldn't pass up farming the rich soil of the bottomland. Although the dam had never failed, the people of the valley took the warnings seriously and by now they had moved people, livestock, and as many personal belongings as possible to higher ground. Jack could not believe his luck. With the exception of himself, and a reporter for a local paper in

Garfield, who didn't even have a camera, there was no one else covering this story.

Suddenly, there was a loud cracking sound that could be heard above the roar of the water. At the same instant, all the horns in the valley started blaring continuously. The cracking sound was followed immediately by the whole center section of the dam blowing out. Thanks to the sports action feature on his camera, that allowed it to take a group of pictures one after the other in rapid succession, Jack was able to capture the entire event on film. The roar became even louder as the water rushed through the gaping hole. The catwalk that Jack had thought about using to photograph the dam was gone, as was the parking lot where he had parked when he first arrived. Thankfully there was no loss of life, not even livestock, due to the early warning system and the due-diligence of the people downstream from the dam. Because only the middle section of the dam failed, the property damage was only minimal. It was a good day all around.

Lead Investigative Reporter. That is how the sign read on the door of the corner office occupied by one Jack Sloan. Destiny will have her way, and Jack Sloan was destined to be an investigative reporter. The champagne flowed and the party went on all night. Guy and Cheryl had sprung a surprise party for Jack, to celebrate his promotion. They were so secretive that not even Susan knew about it. The Atkins had hired the best caterer in the northeast and a band with no less than four gold records to work at the party. Cheryl even hired a local artist to do ice carvings for the occasion. The gala ran well into the six figures, but Guy and Cheryl were happy to do it. Guy had invited several of the people that Jack worked with, some of the neighbors, and some of Susan's friends from the hospital. All in all, there were close to a hundred people at the party, and the food and drinks were bountiful. The party was on a Saturday, and Guy and Cheryl had convinced Jack and Susan to attend a local arts and crafts fair with them. This allowed the caterer, band, and all of the guests, time to arrive at the Atkins' house and get in position for the big surprise without being detected. The valets Guy had hired for the party did a great job of hiding the cars of the guests around on the back of the house and in some of the neighbors' driveways.

Jack gasped and Susan got a little teary eyed when they arrived back at the Atkins' house and were greeted by the all the guests shouting, "Surprise!" followed by the band playing "For He's A Jolly Good Fellow." Jack and Susan were duly impressed that Guy and Cheryl had been able to pull off something of this magnitude and still keep it a secret. The party started out with copious quantities of finger foods, drinks, and conversation, followed by a four course dinner with the featured entree being a choice of either prime rib or Maine lobster and a choice of flaming cherries jubilee or baked Alaska for dessert. After dinner, Frank Stone, the editor in chief of the New York Sentinel, gave an inspiring speech about Jack's natural instincts as an investigative reporter, and his ability with a camera. Several of Jack's friends and coworkers went to the mic to praise him for his many admirable qualities. Before the mic time had ended, it had turned into a full-fledged roast of Jack Sloan, investigative reporter. It was all done in fun and good taste. After dinner, the band played and the partygoers enjoyed dancing under the moonlight or just sitting around talking. Jack and Susan made it a point to personally thank everyone who came. They couldn't remember ever having a better time.

The Army Corp of Engineers asked the paper for permission to use the photographs that Jack took of the dam failure, so they could analyze what went wrong in hopes of preventing such an event with other dams of the same era. Jack's photos of the dam breach mad it to the Internet. They were picked up by the foreign press, and were even used on a television show about disasters.

Thankfully, despite the jaw dropping pictures of the dam breach, a much greater disaster was avoided by the early warning system.

Jack got to pick which stories he would report on, and he was in charge of doling out the assignments to the rest of the reporters. He remembered his start, and would always allow a new reporter to stretch his or her wings on stories that were right at the top end of their ability. This practice sometimes came back to bite Jack in the butt, most of the time it helped the reporters grow. As a result, The New York Sentinel soon got the reputation as the place you wanted to work, whether you were fresh out of journalism school, or a seasoned professional. Consequently, the paper, and more specifically, Jack, got the pick of the litter, anytime a new reporter was needed.

It's funny how life works; Guy and Cheryl owed their lives to Jack and Susan for rescuing them from the Venezuelan jungle. No amount of time or distance would ever make them forget that. Then Guy stuck his neck way out to land Jack his job at the paper, but he felt it was the least he could do. Now it was Jack who felt obligated to Guy for his new title, "Jack Sloan, Lead Investigative Reporter." Jack had been lost, but now he had found his true passion in life thanks to his good friend Guy Atkins.

Guy and Cheryl didn't have to do what they did. Guy could have just offered Jack and Susan a handsome reward for finding them and gone on with his life. Or he could have set Jack up in some bow-dunk little paper in the Florida Swamps. Instead, he took a third option and gave Jack a shot at his dream job. The four of them became friends for life and Jack may not realize it even today, but Guy would do anything for Susan and him. Another thing Jack didn't know is that the following would be his last entry in the daily journal he kept at the New York Sentinel.

The date June 2, 2020: Not much going on in the newsroom today. The sky is overcast and it feels like rain. I've decided to go over to New Jersey and report on a Longshoreman's strike. Maybe I'll take a photographer with me. You never know what might happen.

MAD-MAN IN MANHATTAN

Jack Sloan, Lead Investigative Reporter. That was my title at the New York Sentinel, until a two megaton nuclear device was set off right in the center of Time Square. Ever since that day, I have made it my life's work to find out who did it and who paid for it. The blast happened June 2, 2020. I was on assignment in Jersey covering a Longshoreman's strike. I remember that day as though it happened ten minutes ago. Spanky, a photographer who had come along for the ride, was snapping some shots of the picketers and I was interviewing one of them. When, all of a sudden the gloomy, rainy, day became as bright as a hundred strobe lights going off in my face. Fortunately for us, there was a ship and a large warehouse directly between us and the explosion. Some of the men just stood around like they were waiting for an invitation, but not me. My training as a Navy SEAL kicked in and I grabbed Spanky and a couple of other guys that were close, and we all jumped in the water between the wharfs. The water was dirty and it had a thin sheen of oil on it, but it was better than the alternative. We had no sooner broken the surface of the water when the shock wave hit. My ears felt like I had just dove to a depth of sixty feet below the surface without equalizing the pressure. Then the debris started hitting the water all around me. There were things the size of refrigerators landing within inches of me. I held my breath for as long as I could before resurfacing. When I did, I gasped involuntarily and almost drowned at the sight. The ship, the warehouse, and most of the steel reinforced concrete wharf had vanished. What was left was on fire, along with half of Newark. Of the twenty or so men that were on the wharf with Spanky and I, only four of us made it. Unfortunately, Spanky wasn't one of the lucky ones. The water was twenty feet deep and dark as a tomb, so there was no use in looking for him if he didn't resurface. After a few minutes of treading water and calling his name, I gave up.

When I reached shore, I was greeted by several people, including the guys who had been in the water with me. They were all looking awe-struck in the general direction of New York City. I turned around slowly not sure what I would see and really not knowing if I wanted to know. It was the Twin Towers disaster to the tenth power. The sight buckled my knees. As a Navy SEAL in the Gulf War, I had seen a lot of death and destruction, but this was surreal. All of the tallest buildings were gone and most of the rest were in flames. I knew there were a lot of people around the world that didn't like us but this was beyond any civilized man's comprehension. It's funny how you will struggle to remember the face of someone you once loved, but a scene like this you can never forget no matter how hard you try. After what seemed to be hours, I got myself together and headed off in the direction where I parked my Jeep Cherokee. I'd parked it on the other side of a large mound of dirt, and except for looking like it had just driven across the Sahara Desert, it was in fine shape. I had left my laptop under the front seat, and to my amazement, it still worked. I decided to keep a journal of my activities starting that day.

First things first, I had to get to Susan. She wasn't working that day so there was a chance she might not have heard about what had just happened until I got home. My cell phone was toast after taking a saltwater bath, but I imagined that, despite the fact that they freed up hundreds of frequencies for the emergency responders in 2009, the phone lines would still all be tied up.

Guy and Cheryl Atkins were in Hawaii that week, so I didn't have to worry about them. Guy would normally be working in the city, but Cheryl and he were at a convention on the Big Island. If anything happened to either of them, or Susan, I don't know what I would do. The four of us had been friends for close to ten years and our friendship was and is like fine wine. It just gets better with age.

The first five or ten miles were like driving through a war zone. There was debris all over the streets. Some of it was on fire and some of it was the size of small trucks. The people I encountered were either walking around aimlessly or just sitting on their stoop staring dumfounded. Susan was napping when I got home and had not heard of the events that had occurred in the morning. After getting in touch with Guy and Cheryl, Susan and I spent hours just holding each other. The time had come to talk. I needed to discuss my options with Susan. The way I saw it, I had three options: I could just stay in the Hamptons with Susan and forget about my job in the city, or I could write about what I had witnessed and sell it to the highest bidder, or there was a third option. I could start digging and find out just who was responsible for this horrific act. We really didn't have to think about it. As an investigative reporter there was no other choice but the third option.

So, here I am, five years later and until a few weeks ago, not a damn bit closer to solving the "who done it" than I was the first day. Susan has been very supportive throughout this whole thing, and thanks to Guy's financial support and his international contacts, I've been able to talk to people and go places that would have been out of my reach without him. I put feelers out all over the web, but either no one knew anything or no one was talking. A CIA operative in Morocco was looking promising for a while but it turned out that all he was trying to do was bleed money out of us. Just when I thought this crime would never get solved, I got this email from a computer cafe in Brussels. It was pretty vague, except for a reference to a Mosque in Baghdad. At first, I thought to myself that they might as well have said the answers were on the moon, but it was the best lead we had.

Traveling in and out of the United States, for the last five years, has been all but non-existent. Between Guy's government contacts and some friends of mine that had climbed the ranks in the Navy SEAL program, I was able to not only get a visa to go to Iraq, but I was assigned a squad of Navy SEALs to keep me company in case there was any trouble.

Baghdad sure has come a long way since the civil wars of the early two thousand teens. It's a prosperous metropolis and fast becoming a commercial crossroads of the world just as it was in ancient times. Enough chitchat, our APC also known as an Armored Personnel Carrier had just pulled up in front of the mosque in question and we were about to make our egress. All was quiet as we entered but then again, it seemed just a little too quiet. Out of the corner of my eye, I saw it. Then I heard someone yell "Grenade!" You never saw so many Yankee asses pointing toward Mecca and hitting the dirt. Sergeant Thompson, "Gunny" to his friends, snatched the grenade and chucked it back in the direction it came from faster than a rattlesnake striking a dog.

One thousand one, one thousand two, ka-boom! The grenade went off followed immediately by the sound of Yankee lead. There would be two less jerks walking the streets of Baghdad that night. The score was GI's two, bad-guys nothing. Fortunately, we planned our arrival in between prayer times or there could have been a real blood bath.

The email said something about the third vase on the left as you face Mecca. That made no sense at all until right then. The walls on either side of the Mosque had flower vases hanging on them.

Let's see, if Mecca is that way, then this must be the side I need to look at, I thought. I quickly made my way across the room and snatched the vase off the wall. I emptied the flowers out, but could see nothing. There was a crowd gathering, so time was of the essence. I stuffed the vase under my jacket and signaled the guys to saddle up.

Thank God the crowd had not become a mob and our vehicle was still in one piece. We executed a quick escape and headed back to base.

We thought we were home free when an RPG passed within inches of our windshield. The soldier on the fifty caliber machine gun mounted on the roof opened up on the guy who had fired the rocket. A few of the insurgent's buddies decided to get into the act and before long we found ourselves drawing fire from all sides. Gunny had the driver pull down an alley and everyone bailed out of the vehicle.

I was just about to jump out when Sergeant Thompson stopped me and asked me what I thought I was doing.

"Come on, Sarg. I'm a former Navy SEAL and my war injuries don't stop me from firing a weapon."

"Ok Captain, but if you get hurt I'll never hear the end of it."

"There are going to be some people hurt today, but it's not going to be me."

The sergeant grabbed one of the new M25's out of a locker under the seat and handed it to me. What a sweet gun. It only weighed half of what the M16's use to and it could see and shoot around corners.

Ten minutes and nine insurgents later the battle was over. I managed to pick one of them off of a roof down the street. With the laser range finder and five power scope it was almost too easy. I have got to get one of these guns, I thought, as we all piled back into our vehicle and headed for the base. You wouldn't think a person would miss combat, but at that moment I realized, I did. There is just no adrenalin high like the one you get just after a short fire fight.

After returning to base and getting debriefed about the mission I spent several hours of fruitless examination of the vase. Then I had a brainstorm. I made my way over to the medical building on the base and persuaded the X-ray tech to shoot a couple of pictures of my infamous vase. Eureka! Sealed in the wall of the vase was a key. I wasted no time breaking the vase and recovering it. I recognized the key instantly. It was to a New York City transit authority locker. The only question in my mind was, was this a pre-nuke or post-nuke locker key? Most of the subway system in the city had been destroyed in the blast or buried under tons of rubble. At any rate, my job was done here, and might I say I wasn't too upset about that.

Two days later and I was back in the States. I'm glad the French decided to help us reconstruct the Statue of Liberty. The harbor just looked so empty without her. Fortunately, the device used to destroy Manhattan was not a dirty bomb. It had left a significant amount of radioactive material around, but nothing compared to a dirty bomb. After a three-year clean-up effort by the city, state, and federal government, the city was deemed safe to work and live in. It was recommended that anyone spending more than two hours a day in Manhattan proper wear a radiation detection badge in case they came across a hot spot that had not been completely cleaned up. With the typical New York City attitude, people went about their business griping and moaning but getting it done. The powers that be, decided to start rebuilding the least damaged areas first, and work their way towards the heart of the city. The outer boroughs were the first to get fixed. Not one of them had escaped damage. The New Jersey shoreline including Coney Island, the port, the shipyards, and the surrounding neighborhoods had sustained significant damage too, but that is another story. The first borough to be restored was The Bronx, then Brooklyn, Staten Island, Queens, and finally, Manhattan. It has been estimated that the whole city will be done by 2050, costing between six hundred billion and a trillion dollars.

Talk about cost, that little scrap in Bagdad cost me copious amounts of TLC and a lobster dinner before Susan would let me off the hook. I had told her about my days as a Navy SEAL in the Gulf War. She had managed to pry more details out of me than I had ever planned on telling her, so she knew how quickly things could go wrong and what could happen if they did. Armed with that information, she basically had me over a barrel. Well, all's well that ends well and we ended up on the Fair Winds for the weekend. The seas were smooth and the wind was light so the forty-two-foot catch practically sailed herself. This was good because being on the Fair Winds always makes Susan amorous and I literally had my hands full.

*****

I was surprised how easy it was to locate the locker in question. The Transit Authority was able to tell me which station it was in, and luckily for me, it was not affected by the blast of 2020. The moment of truth was upon me and I was as anxious as a teenage girl about to go on her first date.

A million thoughts raced through my mind as I was putting the key in the lock, including, what if the locker was booby-trapped?

Well I've come too far to turn back now, I thought. One, two, three click. So far, so good Come on baby, don't blow now. It's open and I still have my head. That's a good sign.

Guy and Susan had both tried to talk me into letting the police take it from here, but I'm a reporter at heart. This could literally be the story of the millennium and they would have me just give it over to the police. I think not! Just think about it. Jack Sloan, reporter turned detective, solves the crime of the ages. The crime that neither the police, the Government, nor Interpol could solve, and I did it.

"Slow down Bucko. You haven't solved anything yet."

Talking to myself sometimes helps me get my head out of the clouds. It's true that this could have been a wild goose chase. Elaborate though it may be, still, a wild goose chase. Was it pure Folly on my part, or was it my destiny to choose the third option? Time would be the judge, and I could only wait and watch for the answer. There, in my hands was a manila envelope that might hold the answer to the questions the whole world has been asking for the last five years. Who nuked New York City, and why? Here goes nothing. The envelope was open. There seemed to be a bundle of documents and a letter explaining what they were all about.

Oh, my God! If I can believe what is in this envelope, it will rewrite history as we know it; at least the history of the twenty first century. I went home using a series of turns to make sure I wasn't being followed. When I arrived home it was two forty-five in the afternoon, I went to the dining room and spread out the documents and the letter on the dinner table. I started studying them to see if my initial assessment was right.

Susan arrived home from work around three and helped me sort through the paperwork. According to the documents, and I must say, they looked authentic, the Iranian nuclear program was much more advanced than anyone in the U.S. Government ever knew. It seems that the nuclear plants that the U.S. and our allies knew about were just for show. The real uranium enrichment plants were located under some of the countries hundreds of mosques. According to the documents, on or about August 1, 2018, the Iranians sold a fully functional suitcase size nuclear weapon to a German arms dealer named Schultz Hagen. He, in turn, sold the nuke twenty months later to one John Smith, a former American nuclear physicist with the Los Alamos Research Laboratory.

In May of 2019, John Smith was passed over for a promotion. He apparently led a pretty mundane life until he met someone in a chat room on the web who sympathized with his pain over not getting promoted. They chatted online for about six months before they met in person. The person on the other end of the line was Bill Wilson, a known member of the Patriots for a Free America or PFA for short. This group had been linked to several civil rights crimes and an attempted bombing of a U.S. Post Office. Bill and John met at a bar just around the corner from the local police station. Bill Wilson had been under investigation for anti-American activities by both the local authorities and the FBI. So when the authorities took a picture of John and Bill together, John was immediately terminated from his job at Los Alamos. At that point, John was like putty in Bill's hands. Bill convinced him that the only way to get back at the government was to do something really big. Apparently, the Patriots for a Free America had been in touch with Schultz Hagen, and when they found out he was in possession of a nuclear device, a plan was hatched. They would have John Smith drive to Canada. Once there, he would catch a private jet to Frankfurt, Germany where he would buy the nuke for a cool two mil from the arms dealer. Then, he would return the same way he went, under the radar of course. From there, he would drive to the heart of Manhattan. Once there, he would make an unmistakable statement. John bought into the plan lock, stock, and barrel. Ever since being passed over for the promotion, he had been making a series of bad decisions, one after another. The plan went off without a hitch, unfortunately.

Armed with this information, the FBI was able to infiltrate and take down the PFA. The German authorities were able to apprehend Schultz Hagen and charge him with crimes against humanity. The Iranian nuclear program has been set back by years due to a series of unexplainable mishaps at certain Mosques in Iran. They just seem to implode and fall into the earth, thanks to our friends in the Israeli secret service. Only after the PFA had been taken down did the author of the letter I had found in the packet of documents come forward. It turned out that Mr. Jeffery Douglas was the former secretary for the PFA. When he saw what happened in New York City he suddenly grew a conscience and figured out a way to get the information to me. Even though he wanted the people responsible to pay, he didn't trust the Police enough to give the info to them. The FBI decided Mr. Douglas was just a minor player in the PFA so they didn't pursue his extradition from Belgium.

Once the whole affair was over and done Guy Atkins invited me to go on Safari with him in Africa to which I said, "Thanks but no thanks." He then suggested we go skiing in the Swiss Alps. Again, I just said, "No thanks Guy."

"Guy, I said, I'm going to take option number three and stay home with Susan. I've had enough adventure for a while. Besides, the New York Sentinel is about to start up again and they want me to write a series of articles about my experience."

"Okay Jack, but next spring, how about, Susan, You, Cheryl, and I sailing to the Caribbean on the Fair Winds?"

"Now that sounds like a plan," I said.

*****

So ends my little tale of woe. This is Jack Sloan saying, "Never, discount the third option."

AUTHOR'S POST SCRIPT

I hope that you have enjoyed reading the third option. Though every part of it was pure fiction, I firmly believe in the third option concept. I know of many occasions in my life where the choices seemed limited to one or two, neither one of which seemed right. Then, as by divine intervention, another option would present itself. More often than not, the third option was the right option. So, though this is strictly a work of fiction and I am but a fiction writer I feel there are some lessons to be learned. First of all, never give up. Secondly, keep an open mind. And most importantly, when times are rough and there seems to be no good solution to a situation, stay ever vigilant for the possibility of the miraculous appearance of the third option.

Until next time, this is Carson Brannan wishing you good fortune and good reading.

www.ingramcontent.com/pod-product-compliance
Lightning Source LLC
LaVergne TN
LVHW020440080526
838202LV00055B/5278